by

ARTHUR ROTH

SCHOLASTIC INC.
New York Toronto London Auckland Sydney

Other books by Arthur Roth available
from Scholastic

Avalanche
The Iceberg Hermit

ISBN 0-590-31241-3

12 11 10 9 8 7 6 5 4 3   2 3 4/9

Author's Note

At the time the events in this story were taking place, there were no telephones, no radios, and no space satellites to track ships at sea. Most sailors were doomed if they were shipwrecked in the stormy waters near the Arctic and Antarctic. Few could survive in the frigid waters. And if any did succeed in reaching shore by lifeboat, the climate was often so cold, the land so barren, that they were not able to stay alive.

There is, however, one account of a shipwrecked sailor who was cast up on a tiny, rock reef in the southern Pacific Ocean. The reef was only a jumbled pile of sea-washed boulders. The sailor's only possessions were the clothes he wore, his pocket clasp knife, and one oar.

The Castaway was inspired by the story of that sailor and his adventures.

A.R.

1

The lifeboat rocked and lurched to the motion of the waves. On all sides the vast ocean glittered under a hot, boiling sun. In the bottom of the boat lay two sodden piles of rags. Slowly one of the piles stirred; a sunburned hand appeared, then a mop of black hair.

Daniel Ross raised himself on one elbow. What was that curious booming sound? He sat up and rubbed his bloodshot, salt-crusted eyes, then peered at the water sloshing back and forth in the bottom of the boat. He didn't have the strength to start bailing again. Anyway, what good would it do? Surely they were doomed.

At the other end of the boat his shipmate was still curled under the pile of tattered garments that helped protect them from the fierce heat of the sun. The faces of both men were burned black from the constant sunlight.

Daniel groaned with pain. He felt more like eighty than eighteen. He glanced around and suddenly saw what was causing the curious booming sound. Not more than a hundred yards ahead a wall of white surf was crashing against a rocky shore. For a long moment Daniel stared at the shoreline before it dawned on him. Land! After three months in an open boat he and Josh had reached land.

Daniel scrambled to the other end of the boat. "Josh! Josh!" he cried. "We're saved. There's land ahead. Come on, we've got to man the oars."

Josh Dayton's head came up and he stared listlessly around. At Daniel's urging he got to his knees and pulled himself to a seat.

"Land? There's no land hereabouts, Dan. You're seeing things. It must be a fog bank."

"Straight ahead!" Daniel pointed. "See the surf breaking on the rocks?"

After a ragged start, the men got their oars moving together and they were soon within a hundred feet of the crashing surf.

"We'll never get through here," Daniel shouted. They brought the boat around, parallel to the shore, and rowed along looking for a place to land. Everywhere they searched they saw nothing but rocky shoreline.

They were so weak they knew it would mean

certain death if they were thrown into that boiling surf. Waves rolled in continually and broke on the rocks. Spray shot thirty feet into the air, shrouding the whole shoreline in waving curtains of crashing water.

"It's just a reef," Josh sobbed.

Daniel couldn't bear to see the disappointment in Josh's face. He looked down at his own hands. The sores on the backs had opened again with the strain of pulling on the oars.

"We've got to chance it," he finally said.

"We'll never get through," Josh argued weakly. "It's a watery grave for sure."

Daniel felt a stab of pity for his companion. Josh had been one of the strongest seamen on the *Catherine*. No sailor had swarmed up the ratlines or danced along the footropes of the ship as nimbly as Josh. But now he was a wasted shadow of himself. The bones stuck out in his face, his eyes were deep-sunk, and his lips swollen out of shape. Daniel knew that he didn't look any better himself.

"We stay out here and we end up in some shark's belly," Daniel reasoned.

"Aye, I suppose."

"There might be food and water somewhere on the reef. There's nothing in the boat."

"Aye," Josh repeated.

"I saw one place we might try," Daniel

said. "A sloping patch of boulders — maybe we can beach her on that."

Josh said nothing, and Daniel realized that his shipmate no longer cared what happened.

"All right," Daniel said. "We'll run her in and pray."

The two men began rowing again. Soon Daniel found the spot he was looking for, an opening about ten feet wide between two large rocky shelves. Inside the opening there was a slope of rounded boulders. If they could shoot the gap, they might be able to run the boat up on the boulders and scramble to safety.

As Daniel got the boat pointed toward shore, a swell caught them, sending the bow rearing to the sky. They braced themselves as the top of the wave came crashing down.

"Pull! Pull! Your side!" Daniel shouted, as a large rock loomed to one side.

Before they could bring the bow around again, the boat rose and dropped off with a sickening lurch into the bottom of a trough. Daniel saw the fright on Josh's face as a following wave curled over, crashed down, and swamped the boat. Daniel found himself in water to his waist. Something hit him in the ribs and he let out a roar of pain. He swallowed huge mouthfuls of water as the driving surf tumbled his body over and over.

A shelf of waist-high rock loomed in front of him through the blue-green haze. He tried to hoist himself up, but his wet fingers couldn't get a grip. Again and again he slid back into the water, until the front curl of a wave caught him and shot him forward, feet first, against the rocks. He screamed with pain and fury. Lashing out, he grabbed hold of one of the oars that had jammed itself between the rocks. Half a dozen following waves broke over him, trying to drag him back into the sea, but the oar held firm and Daniel managed to hang on until his lungs began to work again.

When he could move, he crawled halfway up the rocky slope, dragging the oar with him. At a safe distance from the crashing waves he collapsed, sobbing and throwing up seawater. When his head cleared, he remembered Josh and staggered to his feet. He turned to face the sea. There was no sign of his shipmate anywhere. And no trace of the boat, either. Daniel scanned the shoreline, the surf, the waves. Nothing. He would follow the shoreline of the island. Perhaps Josh had made it to land somewhere else.

With one hand pressed against his throbbing side, Daniel hobbled his way along the rocky shore. Half an hour later he was back where he had left the oar. He guessed that the distance all the way around the island was a little over a mile. There was no trace of Josh anywhere.

Daniel made his way to a rocky knob in the center of the island. It was the highest point around, perhaps fifteen feet above the waterline. He sat down and looked out at the vastness of the ocean surrounding him. He could see practically the entire island. His reef, his whale-shaped pile of rocks, couldn't be more than a couple of acres in size.

Daniel bowed his head and said a short prayer of thanks for a safe delivery from a watery death. Then he took another look around at the flat, empty ocean. He was alone. He stood up and took a sailor's clasp knife out of his pocket. The knife was now the only thing he owned in the world. That and the scraps of clothing he wore — corduroy trousers, a frayed wool jacket, and one linen shirt. He had no boots, having cut them up and eaten them weeks ago.

In his walk around the island he had seen no sign of fresh water or food. He saw no animals or birds on the island. There were no trees, no bushes, no grass, no moss.

The full extent of his plight slowly dawned on him. There was nothing alive on this island but himself, and he was half-dead from the

hardships he had already suffered. He was
the only man left of a crew of twenty-two,
who had manned the bark *Catherine* on a sealing voyage out of Philadelphia.

He was imprisoned on a completely dead
pile of rock in the southern Pacific Ocean, with
little hope of survival. In a few days he would
die and his body would be washed into the
sea to join his shipmates.

With this awful knowledge, Daniel collapsed
on the ground.

— 2 —

When Daniel came to he was so exhausted that all he wanted to do was sleep. But there wasn't a comfortable place to lie down. There wasn't even a flat rock big enough to stretch out on.

For the next hour he hobbled painfully about, collecting armfuls of seaweed until he had a soft bed spread out. Then he eased himself down to examine his wounds. His hands and feet, after months of exposure to salt water, were covered with sores. He had lost all his toenails and his ankles were badly swollen. He guessed he weighed no more than 100 pounds, yet when he left home he had weighed 175.

His lips were puffed out to twice their normal size, split here and there with deep cracks. His tongue was thick and furry, and his gums were swollen and covered with blisters. There were several large, ulcerous sores on his hips, where he had rubbed against the boat, and there was a large, angry bruise on his right side.

The sores on his hands and feet could easily turn to gangrene. If that started he knew he was as good as dead. But if he survived and grew healthy, did he want to go on living like this? He was a solitary man on a spit of rock that probably no one would ever find. Surely he would go mad with loneliness.

Turning his back to the setting sun, Daniel stretched out and pillowed his head on his outstretched arm. He found it hard to get used to solid ground again; his body was used to the lift and fall of the sea. Finally he drifted off to sleep.

Shortly before dawn a light shower woke him. He had no way of catching the rain, so he just lay on his back with his mouth open and each hand cupped at his side. When a little water gathered in his palms, he brought them to his mouth and licked the raindrops from his hands and fingers.

He spread his jacket on the ground, hoping he could suck moisture from it if it got soaked with rain. But when he touched the coat with his cracked lips he found that the cloth was saturated with salt from his weeks in the open boat. Nevertheless, the small amount of fresh rainwater he was able to drink made him feel better — a little more hopeful. For the first time in months he let himself think of home and Susan Martin.

Home was Elkton, Maryland, and Susan was the daughter of a neighboring farmer. Daniel had been courting Susan for several years, but that was all over now, he knew. He forced himself to dwell on her flaws — the crooked tooth in the front of her mouth, and the way she walked with her head down, as though she were afraid of tripping over something on the ground. He did this to stop remembering how lovely she really was. He could never decide whether her eyes were brown or hazel or green. They were all three, he decided, and huge and beautiful as well.

Her hair was honey blonde, the color of ripe corn tassels. Daniel had first noticed Susan when she was fourteen and he was a year older. She had come to his house to borrow a scoopful of flour, and when she left he walked with her along the narrow lane that led back to her farm. He picked wild raspberries from the bushes along the lane and fed them to her as she balanced the scoop of flour in both hands. And because her lips were so red with raspberry juice and because she looked so beautiful and because both her hands were holding the scoop of flour, he leaned forward and kissed her. And then, surprised at what he had done, he turned on his heel and ran all the way home.

After that day, Daniel saw Susan as often as he could make an excuse to visit the Martin place. And with the farms right beside each other, it wasn't hard to find an excuse.

But that was all in the past. Susan could never be part of his life again, even if he survived and got home. He had to forget her, forget that awful fight with his brother, Tom, forget his mother and father, his home, his past.

As he sat up and looked around his few acres of barren rock, Daniel thought wryly that he didn't have much of a future, either. The day was dull and gray, with low, black clouds and fretful winds that held the promise of more rain. Daniel didn't worry so much about dying of starvation; it was dying of thirst he feared. He had seen too many of his shipwrecked mates go that way. Maddened beyond endurance, they had leaped overboard to their deaths.

He got quickly to his feet and half-walked, half-hobbled down to the water, to the stretch of rocks covered with seaweed. There were long, dark brown, rubbery fronds and deep green clumps like lettuce. The purple weed was too tough to chew, but the green seaweed didn't taste bad at all, not nearly as salty as he had feared.

Climbing back up the rocks, he found flat pools of water in the hollow places of large rocks. When he tasted the water, though, it was salty. In days of heavy surf, spray filled up the hollows. Then the sun evaporated the water, leaving salt crystals behind. When rainwater fell it turned brackish from the salt crystals.

Daniel cut a piece of cloth from the tail of his shirt and used it to sop up all the water in the hollow of one rock. Then he rubbed the surface free of salt crystals. Now, the next time it rained, the water should be clear and sweet, unmixed with salt. He built a small pile of rocks to mark the place. During the next hour he discovered and cleaned out ten of these shallow rock pans.

He also found several tide pools, large basins of seawater left behind by the outgoing tide. The undersides of the rocks in these pools were covered with small, white barnacles. He scraped a dozen of them off the rock surface with his knife and ate them, crunching them up, shells and all.

Swimming in the pools were tiny, shrimp-like creatures. They were so small it would take a hundred of them to fill a cup, but at least the island was not completely without food, as he had first thought. There had to be millions of barnacles on the rocks on the island, and with barnacles and tiny shrimp he might have himself a steady source of food — at least a starvation ration.

The work of clearing the catch basins for water had exhausted him. He returned to his seaweed bed. Tomorrow, he told himself, he would explore the rest of the island.

Where was this island of his? Daniel wondered as he lay down. Somewhere in the southern Pacific, he knew; somewhere off the coast of Chile, he guessed. It was a treacherous area of uncharted reefs and unnamed islands. He was probably nowhere near the regular trade routes used by shipping. If his island had seals, he stood a chance of being found by another sealing ship. But he hadn't seen any sign of seals.

Despair gripped him again. He would die before a ship chanced by this forsaken pile of rocks. No one would ever know what had happened to him. And he was the only person in the whole world who knew what had happened to the *Catherine* and her crew.

Daniel closed his eyes and drifted off to

sleep. Sometime late in the afternoon he woke with a start. It was raining hard — heavy tropical rain coming down in solid sheets. In minutes he was soaked. He caught rain in his mouth and some in his cupped hands, but the shower passed almost as swiftly as it had come. In the west the sky already shone pink through an opening in the clouds.

Daniel checked the water holes he had cleared in the rocks. They were all filled with fresh rainwater. He had enough water to last for weeks if he could find some way of storing it. The sea was calm now, the wind had died down, and no spray was flying inland to foul up the fresh water. But the sun would dry it up if he didn't find some way to store it. By the following afternoon it could all be gone.

The shifting wind brought a new smell to his nose, the smell of rotting flesh. Raising his head, he sniffed the air. It smelled just like the forward hold of the *Catherine*, where the sealskins were stored. He looked around at the rocks but saw nothing. Tracing the smell, he walked to one end of the island, and there he spotted the black, humped carcass of an animal cast up on the rocks. The rounded back looked just like a large boulder, which was why he hadn't noticed it yesterday.

As he drew closer, Daniel recognized the carcass of a seal. There were white patches on the flippers and raking, white scars on the back. From the grizzled look of the snout, Daniel guessed it was an old bull, and he hoped it was old age and not disease that had killed the animal.

The smell was so strong that it was all he could do to keep from gagging. He took out his knife, and standing over the dead animal, he raised his arm and struck. The blade sank into the black, oily back right up to the haft.

3

Daniel hacked a piece of seal blubber off the carcass and held it to his nose. Up close it didn't smell too bad. He cut off a small chunk and popped it into his mouth. Even with his sore gums and loose teeth he was able to chew the meat enough to finally ease it down his throat. What he needed to do, before the meat turned bad, was cut it into long strips and dry it in the sun. But first he had to open the stomach.

The rush of gas that escaped when he pierced the stomach almost overwhelmed him. But he grimly stuck to his job. In the stomach bag of the seal he found half a dozen small fish. They were half-digested, warm and slimy to the touch, and he had to force himself to bite into one of them. To his surprise the flesh didn't taste raw at all. The seal's digestive juices and the heat of its stomach had half-cooked the fish.

Sitting down on a rock, Daniel ate the remaining fish. It was the first solid food he had eaten in more than a week. Despite himself, he began to feel the first real stirring of hope. He had water and he had enough food to last a couple of weeks. Was there a chance he might survive?

Daniel worked steadily for the next couple of hours cutting the blubber into long strips and spreading it over the rocks. Then he scraped every last bit of blubber away from the hide. When the sealskin dried, he could use it as a blanket, or perhaps make himself some sort of cape. He flung the head and intestines into the sea. He threw away everything except the blubber and the hide.

Working on the seal brought back thoughts of the *Catherine*, and the ice storm. The ship had been beating through gales for three days, hoping to find easier passage well south of Cape Horn, when the heavy sleet storm overwhelmed them. Every spar and line was coated with a sheath of ice. Despite constant chipping with hammers the ice built up, making it almost impossible to reef or set the sails. Conditions grew so treacherous that the men refused to go aloft.

For hours, the *Catherine* had been drifting through light fog. When a huge ice island suddenly loomed out of the mist, the lookout's cry of " 'Berg! 'Berg!" came too late. The ship heeled sluggishly to starboard, then struck the iceberg. The jarring crash snapped both masts and sent the lookout, who was tied to his barrel hoops for safety, into the sea.

Daniel was coming out of the galley, carrying a copper kettle to fill at one of the water butts, when he felt the impact. The crash knocked him to the deck and a wave of seawater slammed him into the railing. He heard someone yelling, "We have struck! We have struck!"

Sails flapped and thrashed out of control, yards and cordage came crashing down, blocks and braces whistled murderously through the air. Daniel found himself snarled in lines and rigging. A hand with a knife made half a dozen swift slashes and an arm pulled Daniel to his feet. It was Biscuits Molloy, the ship's cook, who had sent Daniel for water.

"They're lowering the longboat!" Biscuits shouted. "Help me get some kegs of water into her."

Daniel and Biscuits rolled out a couple of barrels of fresh water from the ship's stores and lifted the casks into the longboat.

"Hurry, lads! We've little time!" Captain Quigley shouted. "She's going over on her beam ends!"

Daniel clambered over the side into the longboat. Although it was long past sunset, there was still light enough to see by; an eerie white glow was reflected off the giant ice island. As they pulled away from their stricken ship, the men saw her heel over on her side and slowly fill with water.

"She was stove so bad you could drive a horse and wagon through the hole," Starbuck, the first mate, said.

"There she goes!" someone shouted.

All that was left of the *Catherine* was a few trailing spars, a hatch cover, a large tangle of snarled ropes and blocks — a jumbled pile of debris floating on the sea.

Captain Quigley took command in the longboat. He set watches and put George Starbuck in charge of the stores. Then he called the roll: "Davis? Kelly? Dayton? Ross? Creggan? Tallcott? . . ."

Each man answered to his name.

". . . Mather? Joyce? Cross? Bole? Speak up if you're on board."

Silence. Daniel looked around. Bole and Cross had signed on in Baltimore. Hadn't

Cross been in the lookout when they struck the iceberg?

Captain Quigley, a blanket over his shoulders, listed the names of the missing seamen in the ship's log. Beside him, Starbuck held a lighted storm lantern that he had snatched up on his way out of the cabin.

"November twenty-sixth?" the captain asked.

"Aye," Starbuck answered.

November 26, Daniel said to himself. Despite the months they spent in the open boat, the crew had always managed to keep track of what day it was. Daniel had spotted the island on March 5. Which meant that today was the 6th, or was it the 7th?

Daniel would have to find a way of keeping time. Perhaps he could make a calendar out of rocks, or mark the seal hide in some way? Then he thought of the broad blade of the oar. With his knife he could carve lines to make a calendar. Mark the boxes 1 to 31, and carve the initials for each month on the side. With a soft stone, he could circle the proper month as it came up.

In two days Daniel finished the calendar. After experimenting with different pebbles, he found one that left a faint white mark on the wood. Now every morning he could mark that day's square and when he got to the end of the month, he could erase all the marks and start over. He wouldn't know what day of the week it was, but he could always keep track of the date, the month, and the year.

His spirits were so much improved that he decided to work on his water catchment holes. Some he was able to deepen. To others he added large, flat rocks to increase the total area of his rain-collecting system. Where he could, he covered the holes with flat rocks to slow down the evaporation. But what he really needed, he knew, was a storage tank. Then after a heavy shower he could transfer all the water to his tank, cover it with the sealskin, and not worry about evaporation or flying salt-spray.

One afternoon he found what he needed — a large, square rock about the size of a seaman's foot locker. But could he hollow it out? He picked up a fist-sized rock and pounded the top of the larger piece of granite. Nothing happened. He pounded again. Several chips flew off. He brushed them away and pounded some more. More chips broke off. After half an hour there was a slight but definite hollow in the top of the rock. It would take a long time, he realized, but he was sure he could make a storage tank out of the rock. Even if he did only one hour of pounding a day, eventually he would get the stone hollowed out. Then he would make a scoop out of seal hide to carry the water from the catch basins to the tank.

In the weeks that followed, Daniel kept working on his tank. Slowly the hole deepened. Meanwhile, several showers fortunately kept his catch holes full. His biggest problem now was to find a fresh supply of food. The dried seal meat was running out, and he had discovered no new sources of food on the island.

When he lay down on his seaweed bed that evening and pulled the sealskin cover over himself, he was filled with despair. He had been allowed a couple of extra weeks of life, but it was only a cruel mockery. What made it especially hard to bear was that he was feeling better every day. His sores were almost healed, and he had even gained a few pounds.

If he was doomed, though, he would leave some mark of his passing. He would not disappear without a trace, not after all he had been through. In the morning, he would start to carve, on the other side of the oar, the story of what had happened to the *Catherine*. He would carve out the story, one tiny letter at a time, and then he would plant the oar like a flag. Eventually a passing ship would spot it and bring the news of the *Catherine* back to the outside world.

Daniel couldn't know it, of course, but the following morning was to bring him visitors, and a surprising addition to his food stores.

— 4 —

Early the next morning Daniel woke to a strange noise. For a moment he lay on his back, looking up at the morning sky, at a just-risen sun. Then he heard the coughing grunts again. It sounded like Sunday morning in church, back home.

He got to his feet, quickly snatched up the oar, and headed for the sound. From a distance it looked as though a large section of the island was breaking up and sliding into the sea; big, black boulders seemed to be slithering here and there. When he got closer he saw that the whole north end of the island was covered with seals. There must have been over a hundred of them. They were climbing over each other to find a better place to sun themselves.

Probably because they had never seen humans before, the seals paid no attention to

Daniel. Now and then one would briefly raise its head and upper body to look around, but then it flopped back down again, untroubled. Daniel realized quickly that here he had a large food source. If he swung the oar fast, he might knock out two or three of the animals before the rest took fright. The seals were slow and clumsy on land. He would pick the ones farthest from the water. That way he stood a better chance of killing two or three before the rest panicked and got away.

Daniel made his choice and advanced on a nearby seal. As he approached, the seal lifted its head and grunted. It seemed unafraid. Daniel took another step. Still the animal showed no fear. Finally Daniel stood only a few feet away. He was close enough to reach out and touch the seal's head with the oar. Slowly he raised the oar. Balancing on his toes, he brought it down in a swift stroke. The shock of the blow ran through his arm. The seal's body bounced once, then rolled off the rock and lay motionless.

To Daniel's surprise, none of the other animals seemed to understand what was happening. He advanced on another seal. Again he swung the oar and once again the seal collapsed. Daniel thought of stabbing the two seals to make sure they were dead, but while he was killing them, the others might get away. He decided to stun at least one more.

But one led to another, and there were eight seals lying on the rocks when Daniel approached a grizzled old bull, whose black back was covered with long, white raking scars. Three straight scars made an almost perfect letter H just below the seal's neck.

The old bull turned its head, then humped forward as though to attack. Daniel backed up a couple of steps, then reached forward and scratched the animal's head with the tip of the oar. The old bull grunted, seeming to like the sensation. At this point Daniel decided to spare the animal. It was the first time in months that he had had such contact with another living creature. Besides, he had enough seal meat to last for months. Why kill any more? Anyway, it would be better not to kill too many seals; he didn't want to scare them off for good.

Daniel bled and gutted the eight seals, then drank several pints of fresh seal blood, knowing that the rich liquid would be highly nourishing. It took him two more days, working steadily, to get all the animals cut up. He saved the hides, scraping them clean and spreading them to dry.

It was late May, and winter would soon be coming to the southern latitudes. While the temperature rarely got uncomfortable, even at night, Daniel didn't know what the dead of winter might bring. The hides would give him some protection from the cold, but he needed a shelter of some kind, too.

Daniel began to build himself a stone hut on the highest point of the island. Like most farm lads he could do a little bit of everything. He built the walls almost three feet thick, to withstand the blows of the waves. His dwelling had no windows and was shaped like a loaf of bread. The walls tapered inward, and he used stretched seal hides to bridge the narrow roof opening. The only doorway was closed off with a hanging sealskin.

He also built three walls to enclose a courtyard so that even in bad weather he could sit out in the fresh air, protected from wind and spray. He kept the water tank and the dried seal meat in the hut, and spent most of his time in the courtyard, which was open to the sun on the north side. He even draped several boulders with sealskins, to serve as chairs or tables.

Sitting in the courtyard often brought back thoughts of home, and of Susan and his brother, Tom. Once Daniel had turned sixteen, Tom had been after him to leave home and learn a trade. Tom had taken over the farm when their father had suffered a paralyzing stroke. Tom, four years older than Daniel, wanted to get married, but he didn't want to bring a wife to the house while Daniel was still living there. It was a long-standing problem on farms in those days. The oldest son would take over the land and the younger sons would have to leave home. Some became apprentices at different trades. Others joined the westering movement, going out to the frontier in Ohio or Kentucky, where there was always work for willing hands. Some went to sea on whaling or sealing ships.

But Daniel didn't want to leave home. It would mean leaving Susan. He was afraid someone else would snap her up. But he never suspected his own brother, even though Tom had turned increasingly bitter about Daniel's refusal to go out on his own. He often made sarcastic remarks, such as, "We can't send baby Daniel to Elkton for nails. He's too young to be all alone by himself." Sitting all by himself in the courtyard, Daniel laughed bitterly. "If Tom could see me now," he said out loud.

There had been some truth in the charge that he had been afraid to leave home. If it had not been for that final evening, he would probably still be living on the farm. He heaved a big sigh, stood up, and looked out at the sea. Not a hint of a sail. How much longer would he have to wait? Another two months? Six months? A year? Surely a passing ship would spot him before then?

It was just as well that Daniel couldn't see into the future.

5

Each time the seals revisited the island, Daniel killed a couple to replenish his food supply. But the one seal he wouldn't kill was Old H, as he called the bull he had spared on that first seal hunt. The old bull was so trusting that Daniel could squat down beside him and scratch the fur behind his ears. Sometimes Old H would even thrust his snout into Daniel's lap. Daniel looked forward to these visits with great pleasure. Old H was the only living thing he had talked to since the day he and Josh had found the island.

Then one morning, as he sat braiding strips of seal hide to make a fishing line, he had the distinct feeling that someone was watching him. The feeling was so strong that Daniel looked up, half-expecting to see another person standing in the courtyard or looking over the wall at him. There wasn't anyone, of course, at least not a person. But in the open end of the courtyard there was a strange black-and-white bird that walked with a curious waddle. Daniel's first impulse was to kill it; the meat would make a welcome change in his diet.

As quietly as possible he reached for the oar. The bird was obviously a fledgling. Its short, stubby wings were incapable of flight. But if it couldn't fly, then how had it reached the island? There were no nests anywhere on this pile of rocks. Indeed, Daniel hadn't seen a bird of any kind even light on the island. Once in a while an albatross would fly by, or a frigate bird, but they seemed to know there was nothing on the island for them. If this strange bird couldn't fly, then it must have swum or floated to shore.

Daniel slowly raised the oar. The bird waddled forward another few paces, made a deep bow, and, from its beak, dropped a small black pebble on the ground.

Daniel lowered the oar. How could he hit something that seemed to be trying to make friends? The bird gave another deep bow, thrusting its black, stubby wings out and back from its plump body. Its beak almost touched the ground.

Daniel stood up and made a bow as a thank you for the pebble. The bird bowed back. Daniel bowed again. The bird returned the bow. For the next minute, man and bird kept bowing to each other. Then Daniel, suddenly overcome with laughter, sat down on the ground. It was the first time he had laughed in months.

By now, too, he knew what kind of bird it was. He remembered several of the older seamen on the *Catherine* talking about "pennies," or penguins, strange Antarctic birds that could not fly but could swim and dive better than most fish.

He remembered Silas Payne recalling how one time he had been with a shore party on an island, killing and skinning seals, when a penguin had taken refuge in their tent one night. For the three weeks the men stayed on the island the penguin stayed with them every night in their tent. Silas said that they took the penguin on board as a pet, but it didn't stay long. The second day under sail it jumped overboard and swam off.

"So you're a penguin?" Daniel said.

The penguin bowed.

Daniel walked toward the bird. It didn't seem to be the least bit afraid. He sank to his knees, then stretched out his hand and touched the penguin on the crown of its head. The bird caught Daniel's finger in its beak and wagged it back and forth.

"What will we call you?" Daniel asked.

The penguin let go of his finger, but its eyes never left Daniel's face.

"I know, we'll call you Penny," Daniel said. "It's a sign of good luck to find a penny — so that's your name from now on. You've brought me good luck."

Penny bowed again. Just to be polite Daniel bowed back, then walked out of the courtyard to see what the bird would do. In its curious, side-to-side waddle, it hopped along behind him, stubby wings thrust out for balance. Daniel stopped at a big, flat ledge of rock that was his favorite lookout point. He sat down, drew up his legs, and stared out to sea. "What's out there, Penny?" he asked. "How far away is the nearest land?"

Penny hopped to the edge of the rock, and before Daniel could stop the penguin, it slid off and into the water. In the blink of an eye it had disappeared.

Daniel grew worried when the penguin didn't return. Then he cursed his stupidity for not feeding the animal some seal meat. If he had made some attempt to feed it, it might have stayed with him. But now it looked as though it had gone for good.

A sudden, awful loneliness swept over him. Having another living thing to talk to was so delightful that he couldn't bear the thought of never seeing the penguin again.

She — for Daniel thought of Penny as a female — had made him laugh, and although he knew it was silly, he called after her. Again and again he shouted her name. Finally he gave up, though he continued to search the surface of the choppy water hoping to spot the sleek black head and streamlined body. Where could she have gone? he wondered. Were penguins capable of swimming long distances? It was probably a hundred miles to the nearest land. He dropped his head on his knees.

The nearest land — where was it? That was all he and his comrades had talked about in the longboat — seeing land, and about food. At first it was the cold that had bothered them the most. After several days in the open boat, many of the men had frostbitten feet and hands. Although four men were able to row at a time and they had a fair-sized sail, it took them several weeks to beat northward out of the frigid temperatures that gripped the tip of South America.

Men died almost every day. The first to go was Henry Davis, the ship's carpenter. He had been hit by a falling spar and injured internally. Sometime during their first night in the longboat, Davis had quietly died. The next morning his body, stripped of clothing, was rolled over the side. His clothes were given to those most in need. Three nights later Hall and Jarvis died. They, too, were put over the side, their belongings shared among the survivors.

The food and water situation steadily grew more desperate. They were down to moldy bread and salt pork. But the salt pork only made them thirstier. Daniel had never imagined what hunger and thirst could do to men. When Slattery died one night, draped over Daniel's knees, he had propped the seaman up and pretended he was still alive. The next morning Daniel ate Slattery's food ration. But that was nothing compared to what he had done later.

Daniel lifted his head from his knees and looked out over the sea, hoping against hope to spot a sail. Sometimes he would close his eyes and count to a hundred, and when he opened them, he could see a ship, a three-masted bark, standing offshore, with a long-boat already launched and coming to the island to pick him up. He closed his eyes now and began to count. But it was no use, he knew. No ship was going to appear, and no penguin, either. When he opened his eyes he would still be alone. There would only be that vast, merciless, blue-green desert stretching away to infinity on all sides of him.

At one hundred he opened his eyes, but he couldn't see anything because of his tears.

6

Hours later, as it was getting dark, Daniel went down to the shore again. He was about to sit down on his lookout rock to watch the spectacular sunset, when a black projectile shot out of the water and landed right beside him. Without a sound the penguin bent her head and began to groom her chest feathers.

"You're back!" Daniel whispered, not daring to believe his good fortune. He carefully reached out a finger. Penny took it in her beak and wagged it back and forth. Shouting with joy, Daniel ran over the rocks, followed by his waddling pet. The island now had two survivors and Daniel had his friend back!

In the days to come Penny followed Daniel wherever he went. She loved to visit one long, sloping rock in particular and slide down it headfirst on her plump belly, building up speed by pushing off with her flippers. She would hit the water with a splash, submerge for a minute or two, then come shooting out to repeat the slide all over again. In late afternoon she would usually head out to sea for an hour or so. Daniel could spot her surfacing from time to time and guessed that she was feeding on the schools of fish he had often noticed dimpling the surface of the nearby waters.

He fed her bits of dried seal blubber, but she rarely ate more than one piece. She always returned the extra pieces to him with the same grave, bobbing motions that she used in presenting him with pebbles. Daniel didn't know it, of course, but bowing and presenting small stones was a standard part of a penguin's courting ritual. Penny was really asking him to help her build a nest and share her life.

As time passed, different parts of the island acquired names in Daniel's mind. Seal Land was where the seals congregated, and he gave the name Dayton Beach to the rocky place where he and Josh had tried to come ashore in the boat. There was also Seaweed Beach, where he collected his bedding. One of the tide pools he called North Pool, and the other he named Black Pool, from the color of the nearby rocks. Penny's Rock, where his pet liked to slide, was another place he named, and Lookout Rock was where he sat to stare out to sea.

In the year that Daniel had been a castaway, he had made himself clothing, buckets, and scoops out of the sealskin, and a six-toothed comb out of seal bone. Because he had no way to cure the skins, they dried out stiff and were uncomfortable to wear. Fortunately, the weather was never bitterly cold, even in the middle of winter.

Usually Daniel thought only of surviving from one week to the next, and he was lucky that his food supply was fairly secure. So far the seals had never stayed away longer than a month. But each time he killed one he was reminded of pig-killing day back home. Every October, to give the family bacon and pork to last through the winter, his father killed two young pigs, cut them up, and cured them in barrels of salt.

Daniel was the "stunner" on pig-killing day. He stood at the end of the narrow runway that led from the pens to the yard outside. It was a job that he hated. He fed these animals every day and now he had to help kill them. He realized it was necessary, but with their high spirits the pigs seemed almost human to him at times.

Tom often made fun of Daniel for what he thought was weakness. So for Daniel, stunning the pigs became a test of his manhood. Life, his brother said, was a brutal affair and men had to measure up to that fact. On his first pig-killing day, Daniel was determined to measure up. He stood at the end of the runway, his back to the milling pigs, his legs spread wide, waiting for the first of the pigs they were to kill that day. When he heard Tom shout, "Here he comes," Daniel tightened his grip on the short stonemason's hammer. As soon as the pig's snout appeared between his legs, he clamped them shut and locked his knees behind the animal's ears. The pig was caught in a vise, unable to move forward or backward. For a moment the animal stood still. In that instant Daniel swung the hammer, praying that it would hit the pig's forehead cleanly and knock the animal out immediately. The killing was up to Tom.

Daniel felt curiously calm. At least he had done all right on the first one. The temptation was strong not to hit the peg too hard, but there was no doubt that the animal had been knocked out. It would have been worse if the pig had come to just as it was being stuck with the knife.

Daniel started to move forward to help with the cleaning, when a scream rent the air. He froze. An awful apparition rushed at him — bloody arms raised on high, a knife dripping in one hand, face smeared with fresh blood. The sight was so horrifying that Daniel ran across the yard in terror, pursued by the demon. He tripped at the kitchen door and fell headlong.

At this point Tom decided that the joke had gone far enough. Realizing that he had badly frightened his brother, he lowered the knife and wiped the blood off his face and hands. But Daniel, terrified out of his wits, lay crumpled against the side of the house. Just before he fell he saw Susan's face in the kitchen window and realized that she had witnessed the whole scene — his cowardly flight, his childlike terror, his humiliation. Although Tom later apologized, Daniel never felt quite the same about his brother afterward. He believed that Tom had meant to show him up in front of Susan, even though Tom denied knowing she was in the kitchen.

Forget the past, he told himself, and he spent the whole afternoon trying to shape a fish hook from a small, curved bone about the size of his thumb. He had to carve a hook and a barb at one end and drill an eye at the other end. The more the work progressed, the thinner the bone became and the more delicate his touch had to be. He lost himself in the work. He sanded the hook into its final shape with a small, rough piece of granite. It looked large and clumsy, and the barb probably wouldn't take much of a grip. But it would have to do.

Daniel tied the long seal cord to the hook and baited the point with a piece of blubber. With a separate strip of tendon, he tied a small stone to the line for a sinker. Then he called to Penny.

He was finally going to find out if he could catch any fish!

7

Daniel headed for Lookout Rock, where he often watched fish breaking water just a few yards offshore. "I know there are fish out there," he said to Penny. "I've seen them."

He lifted the end of the cord with the stone weight and lofted it into the air. It hit the water just beyond the breaking surf and sank from view. He sat down with the other end of the cord in his hand, Penny beside him. He reached over to pet her, and she tried to grab his finger in her beak.

"Fish for supper tonight," he said cheerfully. "I'm sick to death of seal meat. Oh, if only I had some bacon and eggs and hot coffee and biscuits fresh from the oven—"

There was a tug on the line. "We've got a bite!" Daniel jumped to his feet. There was another sharp tug and he began to haul in the line. Then it went dead. When Daniel pulled in the cord the hook was missing. For a moment he thought he had failed to tie it on properly, but then he saw where the cord had been cleanly severed, as though it had been cut with a knife. The fish had bitten through it. He needed stronger line. He hadn't even found out whether his homemade hook worked or not, and it had taken him most of a day to carve it. It was useless to carve any more until he came up with a stronger line.

He made his way back to the hut alone. Penny had gone off for her afternoon swim. He was alive all right, he thought, but what good was being alive, if there was no other human around to be alive *with* or *for*? Even a prisoner in jail had the companionship of his jailers and fellow prisoners. But he, Daniel Ross, might have to spend another year on this island, or maybe five, perhaps even the rest of his life. Wouldn't he have been better off to have gone down with his shipmates?

After two weeks at sea, there had been only a dozen men left in the longboat. They had managed to sail their craft steadily north, hoping to strike the shores of South America. The weather had grown noticeably warmer and the men no longer suffered from frostbite. Food and water, however, were dangerously low, and to make matters worse, Starbuck was convinced that someone was stealing bread.

Although Starbuck kept the bread and pórk casks under close watch, stowed at the bow of the boat, it was impossible to keep an eye on them all the time. One night an argument broke out. Uttering violent oaths, Starbuck was pummeling someone on the back and head. The rest of the men stirred themselves.

"I've got the rascal!" Starbuck roared. "Caught him with his arm in a cask. Looky here, hold up your head, you!" Starbuck grasped a handful of curly hair and pulled the slight figure erect, tilting a boyish face to the light of the moon. It was nineteen-year-old Jimmy Coffin.

"Oh, spare me, have mercy!" Coffin pleaded.

His shipmates looked at him with dull and merciless eyes.

"Throw him overboard," Silas Payne muttered.

"If he's stealing our bread, let him go over the side to make up for it," Red Creggan demanded.

Daniel tried to defend Jimmy. He remembered how he himself had pretended that Slattery was still alive so that he could get an extra food ration. And he remembered how

Jimmy had entertained them in the forecastle with his penny whistle. The simple country tunes he played had made Daniel homesick for the christenings and barn-raisings back home.

"Let him miss his food ration for the next three days," Daniel suggested. Then he appealed to Josh, as they were all three about the same age and had often sided against the older men in arguments. "Isn't that fair, Josh?"

"Any man who would steal food out of a shipmate's mouth ought to be food· for the sharks," Alex Kelly shouted before Josh could say anything. The argument went on for half an hour, until the captain said that he would make his decision at first light in the morning.

After the morning's ration had been shared out to everyone except Coffin, Captain Quigley announced his decision. Phineas Quigley was not a harsh man as captains of those days went, but he knew that if they had any hope of surviving, discipline had to be maintained. He had to make an example of the young seaman.

Jimmy Coffin appealed to the captain for pity. "Don't let this happen to me, Captain. Spare my life. Let me stay in the boat and I won't eat any more food. As you have a son yourself, think of him and spare me for his sake!"

Captain Quigley, who did indeed have a son and two daughters back in Philadelphia, found it hard to steel his heart against the youth's appeal. But justice was justice and as long as he was captain, justice would be done. Still, he was moved by the youth's plea. The boat was moving slowly in a gentle breeze and Jimmy was probably in as good physical condition as anyone else in the boat. The captain's decision would not send the young seaman directly to his death.

"As captain, I hereby order that Seaman James Coffin, of Providence, Rhode Island, be cast overboard and not allowed to return to the boat until the sun has set this day."

The others in the boat looked up with surprise.

"I further order that whoever be on lookout duty prevent Seaman Coffin from boarding the boat while any part of the sun be yet above the horizon line."

Three seamen quickly stripped Coffin of his clothes. His penny whistle and a spoon made from walrus bone, Jimmy gave to Daniel. "I thank thee, shipmate, for speaking up for me," he said.

Daniel felt a great surge of pity for the

naked youth. It could so easily have been himself standing there. The captain nodded, and two of the older men rose to force Jimmy overboard. But Coffin, unlike most seamen of the day, was an excellent swimmer. He stepped up on the thwart of the boat and dove cleanly into the water.

Hour after hour his head could be seen bobbing in the wake of the longboat. The sight of that bobbing head would haunt Daniel forever.

But Coffin was gone now, along with all the others. Even the penny whistle and the walrus spoon had joined Jimmy in the ocean depths. Daniel put down the oar, on which he had begun to carve the story of the *Catherine* and her crew. It was time for his evening stroll and final look at the ocean. He couldn't give up hope that one day a sail would appear on the horizon.

8

Daniel got up from his bed in the hut and groped his way to the stone cistern for a drink of water. When he walked out into the courtyard, Penny waddled over to say hello, and they bowed to one another. The sea was as empty of sail as always.

After breakfast, accompanied by his pet, Daniel made his morning tour to see if anything had washed up during the night. Since coming to the island he had found several useful things cast up on the rocks.

Soon after landing he had found a homespun shirt that must have come from the collection of rags in the longboat, and on a recent morning he had found two logs, both about ten feet long, which he used for prying large rocks out of the tide pools. One day, he told himself, he would try hacking the logs in half to make the frame of a raft. This day he found nothing on the rocks and decided to return to the hut and do some housecleaning.

Every three weeks or so Daniel threw out the old seaweed mattress and replaced it with a fresh supply of weed, which he had dried out on the rocks. One good thing about a seaweed mattress was that it had no fleas or lice, the ever-present companions in a "donkey's breakfast," as sailors called the bag of hay they used for a mattress on board ship. He didn't have any rats or mice to worry about, either.

Daniel often wished for the homely sight of a spider spinning a web or an ordinary house-fly buzzing around his face. Oh, if only he could be back on the farm — see his poor father and mother. His father had promised him a hundred dollars on his eighteenth birthday on the condition that he leave the farm to Tom and go seek his living elsewhere. Daniel had agreed. He could buy a team of horses with the money and go into the carting business, or go out to Ohio and homestead a section of land. But his father's stroke had left him unable to speak, and when Daniel told Tom about their father's promise, Tom was furious.

"He never said anything to me about it," Tom said.

"You know what he's like," Daniel said. "He didn't even tell Ma. I asked her."

"I don't know what you want me to do," Tom said. "You know there isn't any money. You're trying to blackmail me."

"If you give me the money I'll go now," Daniel said. "I was promised it, and I want it."

"I told you, there isn't any money. Where would we get it?"

"Borrow it," Daniel suggested.

"From where? You know we owe money all over the place — the blacksmith, the seed store, the mill. The best I can do is give you the calf money in the fall." Every fall the Rosses sold three or four of the calves that were born to their cows in the spring.

"That'll only be about ten dollars," Daniel said.

"If we're lucky."

"That's a long way from a hundred."

Tom shrugged his shoulders.

How stupid the whole argument seemed now! Why had he been so stubborn? Tom was right, the farm could never produce a hundred dollars. While it provided a living, it rarely brought in any actual money. Daniel wished Tom were with him right now. He would apologize for being so stubborn. The truth was that he *had* been afraid to leave home, and the hundred dollars had been only an excuse to hang on.

As Daniel tidied up the courtyard, he automatically cast a look out at the surrounding seas. He looked, then blinked, afraid his eyes were playing tricks on him. He looked again and there it was — a sail — a pale scrap of gray-white color sitting on the horizon line. Because of the distance it was impossible to tell which way the ship was going, or even how large it was. But the thought of rescue sent him into a fever of excitement. He snatched the oar from its resting place. His shirt was already attached to one end. Holding the staff upright in his hands, he waved it back and forth.

"Let her be a Bedford or Nantucket ship," he cried aloud. "Let her be one year out with nary a barrel of oil to show for it. Let her hungry captain have offered a five-dollar gold piece for the first man calling down, 'Thar she blows! Flukes! Flukes!' Let there be twenty men aloft. Let the first mate be up the rigging with a spyglass!"

Despite Daniel's entreaties the ship wasn't altering course. No one on board had noticed his flag or the waves breaking on the reef. Still Daniel waved the oar, stopping only when fatigue forced him to rest.

At one point he climbed up on the hut, hoping the added height would make him more visible. But the sail continued to move slowly along the horizon, as though pulled by an invisible wire.

The hours passed and Daniel's hopes sank. When dusk fell, the slant of the setting sun made it impossible to pick out the ship any longer. Daniel laid the oar down in the courtyard. First thing in the morning he would climb up on the roof. If the vessel were a whaler, she might return on one of her zigzag runs and sail closer to the island.

That night he found it impossible to sleep. The excitement of knowing that a ship was out there, that there might be others, kept him wide-awake. Whatever happened in the morning, sail or no sail, he had a new project. He had to build a tower. He should have thought of it a long time ago.

But perhaps, when morning came, the dawn's first light would reveal a ship under a full spread of sail, making for his island!

— 9 —

When the first faint light of morning crept into the courtyard, Daniel got up and went outside. It was still too dark to see very far, so he just stood there, holding the oar upright in his hands, staring into the void.

The sun edged up over the rim of the eastern horizon, tinging the sea and sky rose-red with its flood of color. Although there wasn't a sign of a sail anywhere, Daniel waved the oar slowly back and forth. He had been foolish to get his hopes up. Finally he gave up looking and marked the date on his calendar. It was December 23. In two days he would mark his second Christmas on the island.

The thought of Christmas sent him into a numb and despairing mood. He was never going to be found; he would be cast away on the island for the rest of his life. So far he had seen only one sail, and that had been too far away for any lookout to notice his flag. Why was he trying to stay alive? Why bother with the tower? Why didn't he just swim out to sea and let the waves take him? Why did he cling to life?

Look at Jimmy Coffin and how desperately he had tried to stay alive, swimming after the boat. Hour after hour the dark, bobbing head followed in the boat's wake. Coffin's persistence had angered some of the crew. They shook their fists and hurled curses at him. When he could, Coffin held on to a rope that trailed from the boat's stern. Twice Daniel saw him clinging to the rope and said nothing. But if one of the others noticed Coffin hanging on, they beat the boy's hands and head with an oar until he was forced to let go.

Somehow, all through that long afternoon, Jimmy Coffin managed to keep the boat in sight. At one point Daniel and Josh appealed to the captain.

"Throw him a rope," Josh had pleaded. "He's suffered enough!"

"Aye, he's surely learned his lesson by now," Daniel added.

But Captain Quigley grimly shook his head. "Not until the sun is set."

Sometime in late afternoon, an hour or two before sunset, the bobbing head disappeared. No one had noticed exactly when the young seaman relinquished his hold on life. Starbuck, standing up once to search the surrounding sea, had simply announced, "Young Coffin is gone. God rest his soul."

Jimmy Coffin had given up silently, making no last-minute appeal to his shipmates. Daniel felt that the captain's grim refusal to relent would bring them bad luck. And sure enough, that night the captain, who up until then had been one of the strongest of them all, went into convulsions. All night, despite Starbuck's attempts to calm him, the captain's arms and legs thrashed wildly. He roared curses on long-dead friends and shipmates and, finally, just before dawn, he called out to his wife, "Catherine, Catherine," and died. Starbuck held a short funeral service, rolled the captain's body overboard, and assumed command. They were down to eight of the original twenty-two crewmen.

Daniel was ashamed now that he hadn't spoken up more strongly on Coffin's behalf. He had been weak-willed and cowardly. He didn't deserve the chance to survive. It should have been Josh Dayton, or Biscuits Molloy, or

Red Creggan, or even Jimmy Coffin who landed on the island, and not Daniel Ross.

He stayed in his hut all that day, determined to eat nothing until he finally drifted off into a coma. But he reckoned without Penny. Several times he heard her calling from the courtyard. She was missing him, he knew. But she would be far better off without him. And Old H might miss him for a while, but the old seal had plenty of company.

If he had only been able to raise the oar higher, Daniel thought, perhaps the lookout on the ship would have spotted the flag. He should have built a tower twenty feet tall and placed his oar on top. Even a tower by itself might have been noticed and excited the curiosity of the captain enough to lower a boat to investigate.

But it was too late now; he had missed his chance. He made up his mind that he was giving up. It was that simple. He would eat no more food, though he would take a drink of water from time to time. Dying of thirst was too horrible.

Hours later he was awakened by Penny's cries. He sat up, bewildered for a moment. Then he dimly made out the penguin's shape in the doorway. He was surprised. Penny had never entered the hut before. She had always seemed afraid of the darkened room. "What is it, shipmate?" he asked.

Penny let out a cry, then bent her head low to the ground, her stubby, black wings thrust out behind her for balance.

"Hungry, is that it?" he asked. "Or maybe you're lonely?"

He got to his feet and bowed back to the penguin. She bowed again and again — quick, almost angry bobs. He had never seen her so agitated before. He followed her out to the courtyard.

"What is it, what's wrong?" He held out his hand to the bird and she grasped his middle finger in her beak and shook it back and forth.

"Did you miss your sliding today? Is that it?"

Again she waggled his finger.

He cut her a small piece of blubber and then ate a piece himself. He had assumed that Penny would be all right on her own, but now he wasn't so sure. Perhaps she wouldn't survive without him.

Penny waddled forward with a small bone in her beak and, bowing low, laid the gift at Daniel's feet. "All right, let's go for a walk while there's still some daylight left," he agreed.

When they returned to the hut, Daniel looked at the jumbled pile of rocks near the entrance to the courtyard. He could start there, he thought, level a spot about ten feet by ten feet, and start to build a tower. At every foot of height he would insert a slab in the wall to use as a step. He could probably make the tower in a couple of weeks.

"All right then, Penny, tomorrow I'll start the foundation," he said. Somehow he wasn't yet ready to die, he thought. For one thing, his penguin wouldn't let him.

"I want to see a tree again!" he said to Penny. "A tree in full, glorious leaf. I want to lie down in a grassy field with the sound of buzzing bees all around me. I want to roll an ear of wheat between my palms and blow the chaff away and count the grains. I want to see cows and sheep and horses again. I want to see another human being!"

That night, before drifting off to sleep, Daniel thought of something else he could do. He could build that raft. And in those half-dreams that come between drowsiness and full sleep, he saw himself sailing the raft. It already had a name, *The Last Chance*. For companions he had Penny and Old H. When there was no wind, Old H would slip over the side and push the raft with his nose. Penny would help out by using her flippers as oars. His last memory, before he fell asleep, was of sailing the raft right into Philadelphia Harbor and a hero's welcome.

10

When Daniel tired of carrying rocks to the tower, he worked on the raft. With his knife he patiently cut the logs in two, then notched the ends of the four pieces to fit each other, log-cabin-style. He made the joints even more secure with seal bone pegs. Over this square platform he attached four sealskins, two layers of two. He lashed the skins to each other and to the frame with thin strips of seal hide. In the middle of one crosspiece, he whittled out a hole just big enough to take the handle end of the oar.

On a day when the sea was flat as a piece of glass, he decided to test out the raft. He pushed it down to the water's edge and stuck the oar in the socket. With strips of seal hide he tied the sealskin sail to the oar.

Penny took a great interest in the proceedings, waddling around, inspecting everything, once in a while letting out a cry and trying to catch Daniel's finger in her beak. Would Penny follow him if he ever left the island? This day, looking down at her, he realized that the question might soon be answered.

Before he set off he got down on his knees and asked God to protect him. Then he sprinkled a handful of water over the platform and proclaimed, "I hereby name you, *The Last Chance.*"

With that, he pushed the raft into the water and swam behind it. When he was about twenty feet from shore, he tried to climb on. His weight tipped the platform to one side, making it extremely difficult to get on board. After half a dozen unsuccessful attempts, he swam to the front and looped one arm around the oar. For a moment he hung there. Penny was swimming around the raft, shooting up out of the water like a miniature dolphin, then diving back down again. Finally he swung one leg up and over the front log, caught the standing oar with both hands, and heaved himself on board. Under his weight the craft rode almost a foot below the water, but he was able to move the sail to take advantage of the light breezes.

Daniel soon realized that his chances of reaching land in such a fragile craft were about one in a thousand. If he just leaned too far to one side the raft threatened to dump him into the ocean, and what would he do for food and water? He would have to unship the mast during showers and hope to catch rainwater on the flat surface of the sail. But would he be able to take down the mast without capsizing the raft?

Daniel got to his knees carefully and caught the mast. He was curious to see how hard it would be to lift it out of the socket. He gave a tug. The oar raised a little and then stuck. He couldn't get a good enough grip. He wriggled forward and tried again. Suddenly the sail swung around and the raft tilted. Daniel lost his balance and along with the mast and sail slid into the sea. Just before he went under he heard a loud crack.

When he came up, Daniel grabbed one side of the raft and hung on. He discovered that one of the crosspieces, weakened by the hole he had drilled for the oar socket, had snapped in half.

He was now about a hundred feet from shore. He was tempted to abandon everything and swim for land, hoping the wreckage would eventually wash up. But he didn't want to lose the oar; it held his calendar and most of the story of the shipwreck. He thought of cutting the sealskin strips that held the sail to the oar, but he was afraid to take the knife out of his pocket. Since his hands were wet, it could easily slip out of his grip and sink to the bottom of the sea. The knife was even more important than the oar. He dared not take the chance of losing it.

To his relief, the whole oar slid easily out of its bindings and he was soon swimming for shore, pushing the oar ahead of him. *The Last Chance*, borne on the incoming tide, was floating back to land. With any luck it would hit the island, or at least come close enough so that he could swim out and retrieve it.

When he reached the hut he climbed to the top of the half-finished lookout tower and planted the oar in its slot. He might as well fly his signal flag for the last few hours of the day. Shading his eyes, he stared out to sea. Immediately he spotted a high shoot of spray. It arched thirty feet into the air, a thin jet of water that blossomed into a falling, umbrella-shaped spray. Minutes later another watery blossom appeared, and this time Daniel could make out the broad black back of a whale rolling in the water. He watched half a dozen whales sport themselves until they eventually disappeared with a last upthrust of their broad, forked tails. If whales were about, then surely whaling ships were close. Nantucket and Sag Harbor captains were notorious for venturing into any waters after their quarry. Perhaps even now, just over the rim of the horizon, a lookout was calling excitedly, "Blows! Blows! Thar blows!"

That night Daniel thought over the day's events. He wasn't ready to give up on the raft yet, but it was more important to finish the tower, especially now that whaling ships might be about. With that comforting thought, he finally fell asleep.

—— 11 ——

When Daniel completed the tower, it was about three times his own height, or eighteen feet. On top of the tower he had a stand to hold the handle of the oar, and every morning he climbed up to look for passing ships. He repeated the climb several times a day and made his final search just before sunset, when he removed the oar and stored it in the courtyard until morning.

He no longer wore a shirt, but kept both his own and the homespun shirt that was washed up on the rocks to serve as flags, stiffening them on windless days with two thin pieces of seal rib. The shirts, bleached almost white by the sun, were the only suitable things he had for a flag. The sealskin was too heavy and awkward, and it was too dark to be seen at a distance. He could not fly the flags on very windy days, however, for the constant flapping would tear the cloth to shreds.

One afternoon, as he and Penny were sunning themselves with the seals, Daniel was reminded of the hot August day of the McIntyres' barn-raising. Daniel often met Susan at one of those social gatherings that brought the whole farming community together — weddings, christenings, barn-raisings, and even funerals.

There were about thirty men at McIntyres' that day. With horses, block and tackle, and lots of muscle and manpower, they had succeeded in raising the frame of the barn and tying it all together with long ridge beams. Afterward, the men sat down to a picnic supper, served in the open air at long plank tables.

While the men were talking, Daniel watched Susan and another girl clear away the dishes. When they were through, he followed Susan and caught up with her just as she was about to go back into the kitchen. He reached out and gave a tug at the knot that held her apron strings. The knot gave and the apron shook loose out in front of her.

"Your apron's untied," he said.

Laughing, she spun around and aimed a playful slap at him. He danced back out of range. "Someone should teach you manners," she said as she retied the apron.

"You're hired!" he answered. "Come for a walk and give me my first lesson."

"I can't. They need me in the kitchen."

"Away with you!" he scoffed. "There are a dozen women in there already. You won't even be missed." He held out his hand. "Come on."

She cast a last look through the kitchen door, then caught his hand. He led her to the corner of the field where the McIntyres' well was located. It was a nice, cool spot, surrounded by moss-grown rock and arched over with honeysuckle vines. They sat down on the bank, the open well at their feet.

"You realize," he said, "that I've known you for almost two years?"

She caught up a handful of grass. "That long?"

"Remember the scoop of flour you borrowed?" he asked.

"That's when I knew you liked me," she said. "I was so surprised."

"Surprised?"

"When you kissed me," she said. "Remember?"

"I did *not* kiss you." He pretended to be indignant.

"Yes, you did, and my mouth was full of raspberries. I nearly sprayed you with raspberry juice."

He laughed, then leaned toward her to kiss her again.

She drew back. "Don't, someone may come."

"What do I care?"

She reached forward to pluck a small wood chip out of his black curly hair. This time he did kiss her.

She broke away. "Are you and Tom getting along any better?" she asked.

"Not really. He still says there's no money to give me, and I still say I won't leave unless I get my hundred dollars."

"But supposing Tom is right? Supposing he doesn't have the money?"

"Then he'll have to sell the farm and give me half."

"But what will he do to make a living once the farm is sold?"

"What will *I* do to make a living if I leave home?" he asked. "He doesn't care what happens to me. Why should I care about him?"

"Oh, why does it have to be such a problem?" she said.

"If he gave me the money," Daniel insisted, "I could buy a team of horses and become a carter. There's good money in hauling freight. Then, with my own business, I could afford to get married. That's if I can ever find a woman who will have me."

"Oh, you'll have no trouble, you'll be snapped up right away."

"Would you snap me up?" he said.

"I don't know if I'd want a man who's afraid to leave home," she joked.

"Now you sound just like Tom."

Before she could say any more there was a shout from the top of the field, and half a dozen young boys and girls came running down with buckets. More water was needed for washing up in the kitchen.

Daniel got up from the rock and called to Penny. How Susan felt about him should have been clear that day. He just didn't want to see it. She had taken Tom's side against him several times. And why not? Tom was a good catch — a strong, good-looking young man with his own land to farm.

And yet there had been something strange

about the evening he caught them together, something that didn't quite add up. Ah, well, no doubt they were married by now. How far away it all seemed. And how unimportant. And yet, he had actually wanted to kill his own brother that last evening he spent at home.

along the shoreline, the islands there were lava
now above the surface of the sea; one, two,
six along they went out into the cold ocean
far away; it all seemed, but how "primitive."
And sometimes on a more...
far too distant it must to these...

—— 12 ——

In one month of furious activity, Daniel built
a stone wall around his hut, finished carving
the story of the *Catherine* on the blade of the
oar, and repaired the raft. Here is what he
wrote on the oar:

I, Daniel Ross, of Elkton in Maryland, sailed from the port of Philadelphia in 1809, on board the brig *Catherine*, bound for the sealing grounds off
South America, and was cast upon this
desolate island the March following,
where I erected a hut and lived a num-
ber of years, subsisting on seals, I being
the last to survive the crew of said brig,
which ran foul of an island of ice and
foundered on the 26 of November, 1809.
I earnestly request that information of

my fate and that of my shipmates be
made known to our friends in America
by whosoever should find this oar.

Daniel got the stone wall built just in time,
for not too long afterward a bad storm struck.
All afternoon the wind had been rising while
the sky turned a dirty gray color. He took the
oar down from the tower early and made
what little preparations he could. In late afternoon Penny disappeared. She seemed to have
a sixth sense about storms and usually swam
out to sea before they struck. He supposed she
was able to ride out the storms better at sea
than on land. The seals weren't on the island,
either, so he didn't have to worry about Old H.

He piled his store of sealskins in a corner
of the courtyard and weighted them down
with heavy rocks. Then he retreated to his
hut for the night. He got little sleep, however. Hour after hour the wind screamed
around his hut. The noise was incredible.
Waves smashed against the outside wall like
battering rams, and sometime around mid-
night a new sound came to terrify him. It
was a hollow pounding on the roof, as though
some giant hand were slapping the taut sealskins with an open palm. The waves were

actually breaking over the roof of his hut. If the storm got much worse, the force of the water might sweep everything away. Water, pouring in through leaks in the roof, flooded the hut, and he feared that he might be forced outside by the rising water.

But at dawn the wind died down. When Daniel went outside the first thing he noticed were the fish stranded in the courtyard. He gathered them up and threw them in a corner, intending to clean and dry them later.

When he went outside the wall, he found that nine-tenths of his island had disappeared. Seal Land was completely underwater, and so was Penny's Rock and all the other familiar landmarks. The only thing left above water was the bit of high ground where the hut and the tower stood. He was thankful now that he had built the wall. Without it, he knew the hut would never have stood up to the pounding waves.

The air suddenly grew still, and a curious hush settled over everything. The early morning light was flat, a dead yellow. Daniel realized that he was in the eye of the storm, no ordinary storm but a hurricane. Half an hour later the skies darkened again. The wind rose to a howl, and driving rain began to sweep in over the island in horizontal sheets of almost solid water.

Once more Daniel retreated to the hut. From a dozen places in the roof, seawater started pouring through. Daniel could only hunch his shoulders and let it run off his sealskin poncho.

It was like the time in the open boat when they had run into a bad storm. Starbuck was in command. They were completely out of food and had almost no water left. Everyone was very weak; it had been ten days since their last bite of food. The men lay huddled in the bottom of the boat. Only now and again did one of them halfheartedly pick up a bailing tin and empty some seawater over the side. The rough seas and steep waves made it hard to keep the boat headed into the wind, and more than once it threatened to capsize. Fearful that he would lose the mast, Starbuck ordered it unshipped. As he and two others started to take the mast down, the ropes around the sail loosened and the canvas bellied out with a snap that sounded like a pistol shot. The sail, the mast, and the three men went overboard.

Because they were running before the wind, it took Daniel and Josh half an hour to get the boat turned around. They tried to row back, but the seas were mountainous and the other survivors too weak to help or even keep much of a lookout for their lost shipmates. In the morning the men searched the still-heaving seas but could find no trace of the three missing sailors.

The five survivors were in pitiful condition. They had no food and no water. They had already cut up their belts and shoes and chewed the scraps of leather for whatever bit of nourishment they might hold. Now the sail, their only means of obtaining water from passing showers, was gone. They were too weak to man the oars, except in the worst of emergencies. Half the time they didn't know if they were drifting north or south, east or west.

The day after the storm, Silas Payne stumbled his way to the stern of the boat, bowed his head for a minute, then tumbled into the water and sank from sight. The others looked at one another in horror. How long would it be before they followed Payne? A day? Two days? Even now Red Creggan, unable to bear the torment any longer, was drinking seawater. That would soon drive him mad with thirst.

Inside the battered hut, Daniel fought against the memory. The wind seemed to be dying down. Perhaps the storm had blown itself out.

─── 13 ───

Daniel went outside and found that the scudding gray masses of cloud had parted here and there to reveal tiny patches of blue sky. Most of the island had reappeared, though in somewhat different shape, and he knew that his tide pools would be completely wrecked, along with most of his water basins.

Then, between Seal Land and North Pool, a fantastic sight met his eyes!

Resting on the rocks, like the upturned hull of a boat, was the washed-up body of a whale. At first Daniel thought the animal was alive. He approached cautiously, and immediately noticed the trailing rope that went under the body.

He climbed around the animal and found that the rope led to the eye of a harpoon that was sunk full-length into its back. He walked up on the whale's back and tugged at the harpoon. It was stuck fast. He would have to cut it free with his knife. He reached down and cut the rope at the harpoon eye. With some hard tugging he was able to snake it free of the anir al's body. Looping it around his forearm in hand-to-elbow coils, he guessed its length at twenty-five feet. When he unraveled its three strands and tied them end to end, he would have seventy-five feet of rope.

The whale was about thirty feet long, and Daniel spent the rest of the day opening its stomach. He saved the heart and cut some strips of lean dark meat to set out to dry on the rocks. The blubber he did not try to cure. It looked and tasted almost the same as seal blubber, and he already had plenty of that.

But the whale proved to be a problem. Under the heat of the sun, the blubber was soon rotting and it began to stink. Every day Daniel spent an hour hacking loaf-sized pieces of blubber off the carcass and throwing them into the sea, where the fish made short work of them. He wanted to get down to the skeleton, parts of which he felt he could use.

As the whale meat grew more rotten, it got easier to slice away from the bone. One day Daniel managed to cut out a dozen of the animal's ribs. With them, he rebuilt the roof of his hut, using the ribs as a rigid frame. Over the frame he hung an unbroken piece of whale-skin, its ends weighted down with rocks. Now his roof was completely waterproof and no longer sagged in the middle.

He also made use of the backbone. The larger individual segments, covered with seal-skin, made perfect stools. Their hollow cores were much more comfortable to sit on than the hard rocks he had previously been using for chairs. He was delighted, too, with the harpoon. He could use that to stun and kill the seals, instead of using the oar, which he wanted to keep solely for a flagstaff.

It was months before the last of the whale disappeared from the rocks. Daniel had salvaged nearly all the bones and piled them, along with the seal bones, just outside the wall. Once a day he picked out a bone and smashed it open to get at the marrow. He remembered hearing from an old sailor on the *Catherine* that Eskimos never got scurvy because they ate a lot of bone marrow.

Daniel finally had a way to fish off the rocks. Using hooks carved from seal bone and a weighted rock as a sinker, he twirled the end of his seventy-five-foot rope around his head and let it go. The bait sailed fifty feet out to sea, then sank to the bottom. His first catch was a four- or five-pound deep-bellied bottom feeder with a snub mouth.

He had the fisherman's usual problems, though. He often lost the bait, suspecting that crabs were eating the seal meat right off the hook, and he lost a lot of fish because the barbs didn't hold. Weather was another problem — the sea had to be calm enough so the bait would lie on the bottom and not get churned around in rough water.

Taking everything into account, though, fishing brought him eight to ten fish a month, enough to pleasantly vary his diet of seal meat.

Best of all for Daniel was the thought that the harpooned whale was evidence that whaling ships were somewhere in the area. It was a hopeful sign. But as the months passed and no ship came in sight, he began to lose heart again. Sunset was often a bad time. There was something about the purple light, the hushed quality of the air, that filled him with a deep sorrow, a deep longing for home. Perhaps the worst times, though, were when he dreamed that he was back in Elkton, and woke up to find that he was still alone in his stone cell in the dark, in the middle of the ocean. The first time this happened, he tried desperately to get back to sleep, hoping to reenter the world of home. But it hadn't worked. He wound up staring into the dark, listening to the never-ending, dismal crash of the surf on his rocky island.

There was one part of home, though, that he hated to dream of or think about, and that was the day he left for good. It was a Sunday, and Susan was coming over in the evening to visit. They planned to sit in the kitchen and talk with the family for a while before going out for a walk.

After the cows had been milked that evening, Tom said to him, "Can you take the slasher and close that gap in the Indian Field where the split elm is? I'm afraid the cows will break out."

"Can't it wait until morning?" Daniel asked. "Susan will be here any minute now."

"It will only take you five minutes," Tom argued. "Susan will still be here. I'd go, only the milk's ready and Ma is waiting for me to help with the churning."

Daniel got the billhook from the barn and walked out to the Indian Field. He found the hole in the hedge, and with the billhook he cut some birch saplings and set them crossways in the gap. Then he picked out half a dozen nearby honeysuckle vines and threaded them in and out through the saplings so that they knitted in with the rest of the hedge. Satisfied, he shouldered the billhook and started home. It hadn't taken him more than ten minutes.

He was whistling, billhook over his shoulder, as he came back down the lane. He had just passed the barn when he saw two figures at the gable end of the cart house — Tom and Susan, with their arms around each other. With a cry of rage, Daniel raised the billhook over his head. He would cleave Tom in two, from top to bottom.

"No, Daniel!" his brother shouted, pushing Susan away.

Suddenly Daniel realized what he was doing. Horrified, he dropped the billhook. Its wicked meat-cleaver edge rang as it struck the ground. Daniel turned and ran for the house. Bursting into the kitchen, he scooped seven dollars from a pewter bowl on top of the dresser. He thrust the coins — his life savings — into his pocket.

"What's wrong, Daniel?" his mother asked as her son stared around the kitchen. For a long moment Daniel looked at his father, sitting motionless in the chair.

"Good-bye, Father," he said softly. Then he called another strangled "good-bye" to his mother and ran out of the house.

Thinking back over the whole scene now, Daniel realized that there was something very strange about it. There might, after all, have been an innocent explanation for Tom and Susan's embrace. He had never given either of them a chance to explain. Then, too, it was very odd that they didn't hear him. Tom knew that his brother would be coming back from the Indian Field. They should have heard him. If they didn't hear his footsteps, they must at least have heard his whistling. It was almost as though they wanted to be caught. But why? He was sure there had never been anything between them. But then what reason could they have for their conduct? If they had deliberately planned to provoke him, they must have been surprised at his reaction. He had never shown such a temper before. And then his swift flight from home — he had actually run the first three miles of the road, run until his lungs were fit to burst.

Daniel shook his head. He didn't want to think of it anymore. The best way to forget was to throw himself into his work, braid some more seal-hide rope, check the tide pools, gather some seaweed, comb his beard and hair, climb his tower and look out to sea — or talk to Penny.

"Come on, girl, let's walk down and see if the seals are back."

14

In all his time on the island Daniel had never
gotten seriously ill. But one day he woke
feeling miserable. His stomach was a hard
knot of pain and he couldn't eat anything.
When he tried to walk, he found himself
barely able to move. In fact, he felt so bad,
so drained of energy, that he didn't care
whether he lived or died. He felt as bad as he
had during those final exhausted days in the
open boat.

Whole days had gone by then when he only
wanted to have everything over with, one way
or the other. He wished he could follow the
example of Payne and just slip overboard. But
he lacked the courage, or despair, or whatever
it took. By then there were only four survivors
left: himself, Josh Dayton, Red Creggan, and
Biscuits Molloy.

One afternoon Daniel found himself being shaken. He lifted his head and looked into the inflamed eyes and wild face of Red Creggan.

"Ross, listen, Ross. Biscuits is almost dead. He's gone bad. Heave him over, let's heave him over!"

Daniel looked down at the stern of the boat where the body of Molloy lay under a pile of rags. "Is he dead?" he asked. Like most cooks, Biscuits had been a man of considerable weight, though by now most of it had melted away.

"He's as near dead as will make no difference," Red said. "He's a drag on the boat. I'll knock him on the head with an oar and we'll heave him over."

"Heave Biscuits over?"

"With Biscuits gone, there'll be more for us," Creggan said in a furtively pleased whisper. Crouching in front of Daniel, he tugged at the young seaman's arm. "More for us to share, don't you see? Don't you see, more to share."

Daniel realized that he had a madman on his hands. Red Creggan had obviously lost his mind. More *what* to share? They were out of food and water.

Creggan gave a wolfish grin. "The sharks

will get him. They'll strip him to the bone. Help me and we'll tip him over. More for us to share, don't you see?"

"Tonight, later tonight," Daniel said, hoping that in time Creggan would come to his senses.

"We'll dump him over. More for the rest of us." A crafty look crept into Creggan's eyes as he lurched away.

At the stern, Molloy and Dayton were lying motionless under the cast-off clothing of their dead shipmates. Daniel was vaguely aware that Red Creggan was standing up, an oar in his hand. What was the fool trying to do? Daniel wondered.

He closed his eyes again. What difference did it make? They were all doomed. Biscuits was more dead than alive, and all the spirit seemed to be gone from Josh. Creggan was clearly mad and Daniel Ross was — Creggan! Surely he didn't intend to. . . .?

He saw Creggan raise the oar over his head, then brace himself against the roll of the boat. Red was standing over the motionless body of Molloy.

Shout! Daniel told himself. *Warn Molloy. There's still time. Biscuits helped cut you free when the* Catherine *struck the iceberg.* But some awful force held Daniel's tongue still.

Horrified, he saw the oar come down on Molloy's head.

Still Daniel kept quiet. He watched Red Creggan heave Molloy up on the oarlocks. The demented sailor struggled with the body for a moment. Then a downward tilt of the boat, a push from Creggan, and Molloy tumbled overboard. Daniel struggled to his knees. There was still time to throw Molloy a rope. He saw Creggan advancing on Josh, the oar once again raised over his head. Daniel froze, still unable to call out. Was he going to allow another murder?

Finally an awful roar tore loose from Daniel's throat. Josh opened his eyes in time to see the oar falling through the air. He rolled away and the end of the oar bounced off the thwarts.

Daniel scrambled to the stern and reached the two sailors just as Creggan caught Josh around the throat with his hands. Daniel punched the berserk seaman and Creggan went down.

"Heave him over!" he yelled to Josh.

Josh had broken Creggan's hold on his throat. Now he caught a handful of red hair in his fist, bringing Creggan roaring to his feet. For just a moment the sailor was off balance, caught at the height of 'the boat's roll. Daniel jabbed Creggan hard in the stomach with the handle of an oar and the crazed seaman went over the side. Seconds later Creggan's angry red hair appeared behind the boat's stern.

"Good lads," he called cheerfully. "Throw me a rope. I can barely swim."

He sounded perfectly sensible, like the Creggan of old. The shock of hitting the water must have brought him to his senses, Daniel thought.

"Best throw him a rope," Josh said.

"No!" Daniel yelled at Josh. He pointed at Creggan, who was valiantly trying to stay afloat. "He killed Molloy; let him perish for it!"

"Ah, lad, don't do an old shipmate like this," Creggan pleaded, seemingly unaware that he had murdered Molloy and tried to kill Josh.

But Daniel refused to throw a rope. He didn't have long to listen to the pleadings of the doomed sailor. Creggan soon gave up the fight and slipped away beneath the waves.

That night a squall brought them rainwater, enough to quench their thirst. In the morning a large, white seabird perched on the bow and Daniel managed to kill it with a lucky blow of the oar. That kept them alive until they sighted the island.

Daniel still felt guilty when he thought that he might have saved Biscuits and hadn't. He couldn't explain his silence except that he must have been a little crazy himself, crazy with fear that Creggan might turn on him.

Daniel turned on his seaweed bed and groaned. It had to be morning. Was this the second or third day of his illness? He was losing track of the time.

Penny's call came from outside. Daniel didn't answer. He still felt too weak to get up. He heard a scraping sound, then suddenly she was in the hut, looking down at him.

"Go away," he said. "I'm not getting up."

Penny bowed low, her short, stubby wings pointing straight behind her. She opened her beak and dropped a small stone on the ground.

"Thank you, shipmate," he said. "Now, be off with you. Sport yourself elsewhere!"

Penny's answer was five or six trills in a row. He clapped his hands over his ears. The sound was intolerable in the confined space. What did she want, anyway?

When another volley of croaks split the air, Daniel sat up with a mournful complaint. "You're a harsh mistress, Pennybird." He got up just to please her. Maybe if he went outside and took a look around, it would satisfy her.

When he got to his feet he felt better than he thought he would. At least his legs seemed a bit stronger. He stopped for a drink of water, then went out to the courtyard. He might as well put up the signal flag.

He was halfway up the tower when he noticed something bobbing out on the water. For a moment he was afraid to trust his eyes. When he did, he scrambled swiftly to the top and began to shout and wave the oar back and forth furiously.

15

From the top of the tower, Daniel saw a ship's boat with four men inside, making directly for the island. He kept waving the oar back and forth and shouting, though his efforts weren't really necessary. The men in the open boat could see him, and the captain and his mate, standing on the foredeck of a four-masted bark, were watching him through spyglasses.

Daniel climbed down from the tower and ran wildly through the courtyard, almost tripping over Penny. What should he do with Penny? Could he take her? Should he leave her behind? He was so excited he didn't know what he was doing. He had to take the oar; it had his story and the calendar on it. But not the harpoon. His knife, yes. But the less he took the better.

He ran down to the shore to check the progress of the boat. It seemed to be heading toward Black Pool, which was not a good landing place. Still the men would have trouble no matter where they tried to land. The sea was running high.

Daniel watched the men ship their oars when they got within fifty yards of the rocks, turn the boat, and follow the coastline. On shore, Daniel kept pace, leaping from rock to rock, Penny hurrying along behind him. Periodically Daniel stopped to wave his arms and call out to the sailors.

After the boat made a complete circuit of the island, one of the sailors in the boat stood up and shouted to him. Because of the noise of the crashing surf, Daniel couldn't hear what the man was saying. He couldn't even tell what language the sailor was using. But about one thing there was no mistake. The boat was turning around and heading back to the ship.

For a moment Daniel was thunderstruck. Were they going to abandon him? He didn't know it but the men in the boat were going back for a rope and a grappling hook to see if they could get the marooned man off by rigging a line to the island.

Daniel's surprise soon turned to anger. They weren't going to just leave him, the cowards. He would hurl himself into the water and swim after them. Then he thought of *The Last Chance.* He hurried to where the raft was tied and, in a panic of impatience, dragged it down to the water's edge. His excitement got through to Penny and she began to trill excitedly. He looked down at her.

"Well, shipmate, we've come to a parting of the ways." He bent down to pat her on the top of the head and she managed to catch his finger in her beak and wag it back and forth.

"Yes, Penny, I'll miss you, too." He eased his finger free and his eyes began to fill with tears. Even if he were rescued, he couldn't take her on board. She belonged in the sea, with her own kind. Still, she had made his life on the island bearable and she had rescued him by making him get out of the hut, as though she knew that a boat was on the way.

But he had to hurry! The rowboat was now halfway back to the ship. If he got the raft past the breakers, Daniel thought, maybe they would return. If they didn't, he was lost. He could never swim as far as the ship. He waited for a lull between two waves, then pushed the flimsy platform into the water and hung on. The oar rode across the raft. If the raft went down, he could still hang on to the oar.

He made it through the first breaking wave,

then the second and the third. The raft stayed afloat, bucking and heaving in front of him. Daniel kicked his legs, forcing the raft through the water. Ahead of him, he caught sight of Penny's sleek black-and-white body, weaving up and down, sewing stitches in the water's surface. He hoped the men in the boat would not harm her. He had to tell them she was a pet.

A large wave came in and the raft climbed to meet it. Daniel felt the water lift his body. Then he saw the raft tilt slowly up on one edge. He tried to get out of the way, but as the raft turned turtle, one of the wooden crosspieces came down and cracked him on the head. His mind seemed to shatter into a thousand pieces. His body lost all strength and slid under the surface. *Grab the oar*, he told himself, *hang on to that*. Then his last thought was, I'm going to die after all.

The men in the boat had seen what was happening and had already turned back. One of the sailors dove overboard and held Daniel up until the rowboat came alongside, and another retrieved the floating oar.

Daniel was unconscious when they got him aboard ship. The captain of the *Neptune*, which was bound for New York after a trading voyage to the Spice Islands, ordered the castaway put in a berth until he regained consciousness or died.

At first his rescuers thought Daniel was a native of the island. He was burned almost black by the sun, his hair hung down past his shoulders, and his beard reached to his waist. He was naked except for his trousers, which were patched with sealskin in so many places that it was hard to tell what the original material was. But when the sailors saw the writing on the oar, the mystery was solved. Some still argued, though, that the original Daniel Ross had been killed by the wild man they had on board, because no civilized person could have lived so long on a barren island without any kind of food. But then how could a wild man survive? others asked. And the calendar, someone pointed out. Would a savage keep a calendar?

Another mystery was the penguin that followed the ship night and day. Some of the sailors insisted that it was a sign of good luck, while others said it was exactly the opposite. One sailor claimed that the penguin had been following the ship for over a week, but others said that the bird had first been sighted the same day they picked up the castaway. None of the sailors connected the two events or guessed that the penguin had been a pet of the Wild Man, as Daniel was now generally known.

Toward evening on the third day after Daniel had been rescued, a school of penguins was spotted swimming around the vessel. They stayed an hour or so, putting on a swimming and diving display; then, as mysteriously as they appeared, they left. And the solitary penguin went off with them, never to be seen again by any of the crew.

16

Daniel opened his eyes and looked around at the cabin of the *Neptune*. On a dark, smoky beam over his head there were a dozen sets of carved initials: CG, CD, AR, RB. It all came flooding back to him: the boat rowing away from the island, the raft cracking him on the head. He shouted and a sailor entered the cabin.

"My oar!" Daniel said. "Where's my oar?"

The sailor grinned and was back in minutes with the oar. Daniel sat up and set the blade end in his lap. "What day is it?"

"Tuesday," the sailor said.

"No, no, what date? What month? What year?"

"May 10th, 1815."

Daniel looked at his calendar. The last mark was on the first. But he had the month right.

And in the corner where the year was written, he saw his "14" canceled out, with "15" carved underneath.

"I was off by nine days," he said.

"You've been out cold for the past six," the sailor told him.

"And I was sick for two or three days before that and didn't mark the calendar." Daniel shook his head in wonder. "I was over five years on that island. I never thought I'd get off."

"You almost didn't," the sailor said. "If we hadn't been blown off course, you'd still be there."

Daniel was soon up and about and an object of great curiosity to the members of the *Neptune*'s crew. He had to tell his story again and again.

He was taken on as a member of the crew and was to get twelve dollars when the ship docked in New York. The other seamen all got together and between them managed to outfit the new sailor with a complete set of seaman's gear.

Daniel finally arrived back in Elkton with ten dollars in his pocket, and the clasp knife and the oar as the only souvenirs of his five years on the island. He took the familiar road home and was soon walking up the lane to his house. While he was still fifty yards away, a young woman came to the door and, with a sweep of her arm, scattered a basin of water across the yard. She didn't see him.

The woman wasn't Susan. Could Tom have sold the farm? Were strangers now living on it? Daniel wondered as a small boy came running around the side of the house, chasing a hen.

"Dan'l, Dan'l, you stop that right away," came a young woman's voice from inside the house. "You've got the hens scared out of their wits."

The boy stopped, for he had caught sight of the stranger. Daniel could clearly see Tom's features on the child, especially in the intense blue eyes and stubborn set of the mouth.

He put down the oar and walked up to the boy. "Hello, Daniel," he said. "I'm the man you were named after."

Moments later Daniel stood in the doorway of the house. His father wasn't in the kitchen, nor was his chair there, and Daniel instinctively knew that his father was dead. But his mother was there, along with a young woman folding sheets. Daniel didn't know how to announce himself.

The women looked at him, wondering what the bearded stranger wanted.

"Is Tom Ross here?" Daniel said, feeling foolish.

His mother dropped her end of the sheet and her hand flew up to her mouth. "Daniel?" she whispered. "Is that you? Is it you?"

While she hugged him, his mother kept saying over and over again: "Is it really you, Daniel? Is it you, son, at last? I knew you'd come home. Daniel, Daniel, is it really you at last?"

Finally she pushed him away to get a better look at him. "You've lost weight, son. You haven't been eating properly." Then she burst into tears and grabbed him again in a fierce hug. She turned to the other woman. "I knew the voice right away. That's how I knew, the voice. I'd always know that voice."

When she was finally calm, she introduced Daniel to Ruth, Tom's wife, who sent young Daniel out to the field to bring Tom back to the house.

As he entered the kitchen, Tom stared at his brother.

Daniel smiled. "I'm not a ghost, Tom. It's really me, your brother, Daniel."

The brothers embraced, and soon Daniel was sitting at the kitchen table, enjoying a hearty meal and telling everyone of his adventures over the past six years.

Later Tom took Daniel on a walk around the farm. He put a hand on his brother's arm. "Ah, Daniel, Susan and I did you a terrible wrong."

"No, no," Daniel objected. "It's all forgotten."

"You don't understand," Tom said. "There was never anything between Susan and me. We were pretending that night. I thought when you saw us together you'd be afraid that Susan would marry me, and that would make you leave the farm and set up for yourself somewhere so you could win her back.

"Poor Susan agreed with me about provoking you. She saw no future for you and her so long as you stayed home. But we didn't think you would go berserk and run away like that. I finally traced you all the way to Philadelphia and the *Catherine*. But when no word was heard of you or the ship after three or four years, we thought the *Catherine* was lost at sea with all hands."

"Where is Susan now?" Daniel asked. "I suppose she's married?"

"No, she's still at home. She teaches school now."

"I'll go over this evening and say hello."

"You'll do no such thing," Tom said. "Your first day back and already you're running off? You'll spend the evening with us. Anyway, you can see her tomorrow at the church fair."

"Are you sure she'll be there?" Daniel asked.

"She'll be there. She's in charge of one of the booths." Tom laughed and slapped his brother on the back. "But, man, I'll have to introduce you to her. She won't know you with that beard."

As Tom walked with Daniel back to the house, he said, "As you can see, Daniel, I've done fairly well since you left. The crops have been good and I've been lucky with my stock. I've put a bit of money aside. I want you to take one hundred dollars as your share of the farm."

Daniel smiled. It was funny, he thought, but now that he was being offered the money he didn't want it anymore. "I can't take it."

"I want you to have it," Tom insisted. "It's what Pa promised you."

"No, no," Daniel said. "You keep it. If I ever need it, I'll ask for it, all right?"

Tom hesitated for a moment. "All right," he finally agreed. "It'll be your wedding present."

* * *

The church fair was in full swing when Daniel arrived the next day with Tom and Ruth and young Daniel. There were booths selling cakes and pies, others offering jams and jellies. There were dart throws and guess-your-weight booths; but one of the most popular was the kissing booth.

When Daniel was still twenty yards away from the booth, he spotted Susan. He stopped as soon as he saw her. Her long, blonde hair was piled up in a loose knot on top of her head. She was smiling and he recognized the crooked tooth that edged slightly over its neighbor. She seemed less shy than she used to be, he noticed, making jokes and smiling at the bystanders.

"Daniel, you go by yourself," Tom said. "I'll bet you a glass of ale that she doesn't recognize you. We'll stay back here. If she sees you with us, she'll know right away who you are."

Daniel moved forward to the booth, where a young boy was trying to ring one of the stakes with a quoit made out of tightly bound straw. A sign on the booth read: THREE RINGS WINS A KISS. A PENNY A THROW.

Daniel pushed forward and held out a penny. Susan handed him three rings. "Good luck," she said with a flirtatious grin. As she looked at him, a brief, troubled expression came into her eyes. "Do I know you?" she asked.

Afraid to speak, Daniel quickly turned away. He went to the line and lofted the ring. It collared the wooden post. The second quoit also landed true, but the third missed by inches. Several groans came from the onlookers.

"Another try?" Susan asked. She collected the straw rings and brought them over to him with a smile.

He handed her a penny and got ready for another try. His first throw was good, but his second ring caught the top of the post and hung there, neither around the stake nor off it.

Susan shook her head. "Sorry, it has to circle the post."

Daniel took careful aim with the last ring and lofted it into the air. It struck the second quoit, knocking it to the bottom, and suddenly all three golden rings were circling the stake. The crowd cheered.

"Fair's fair," Susan said, walking over. Daniel leaned forward and lightly kissed her on the lips. Then he drew back. "You taste of raspberries," he said softly.

Panic suddenly crumpled Susan's face as she recognized the familiar voice. "Daniel!" she screamed. Then she used the very same words his mother had spoken the day before. "Is it really you, Daniel?"

"It's really me, love, and I'm home for good," Daniel said as he put his arms around her.